The LOUDS Move In!

Chompity Chomp Chomp

by **Carolyn Crimi**   illustrated by **Regan Dunnick**

Marshall Cavendish Children

Marshall Cavendish Corporation
99 White Plains Road
Tarrytown, NY 10591
www.marshallcavendish.us

Library of Congress Cataloging-in-Publication Data
Crimi, Carolyn.
The Louds move in / by Carolyn Crimi ; illustrated by Regan Dunnick.— 1st ed.
p. cm.
Summary: When the Loud family moves into the neighborhood alongside
Mr. Pitterpatter, Miss Shushermush, and Miss Meekerton, things begin to change.
ISBN-13: 978-0-7614-5221-8
ISBN-10: 0-7614-5221-4
[1. Noise—Fiction. 2. Neighbors—Fiction. 3. Moving, Household—Fiction. 4. Humorous stories.]
I. Dunnick, Regan, ill. II. Title.
PZ7.C86928Lou 2006
[E]—dc22
2005002532

The text of this book is set in Filosophia Regular.
The illustrations are rendered in Acrylic paint and charcoal pencil.
Book design by Adam Mietlowski

Printed in China
First edition

1 3 5 6 4 2

mc Marshall Cavendish
Children

For my lovable in-laws, with a special loud SMOOCH to Chickie and Cheryl
—C.C.

To my family, Debbie, Brandon, Tom Allen, and to my good friend, Stretch
—R.D.

Things had always been quiet on Earmuffle Avenue.

The quiet neighbors stayed in their quiet homes doing quiet things.

No one even spoke to each other.

Then one day, the Loud family moved in, and everything changed.

The Loud family walked loud. Stomp stompity stomp. They ate loud. Chomp chompity chomp. But mostly they talked loud. "STOP PUTTING OATMEAL IN THE BABY'S HAIR!" Ma Loud yelled. "WHERE'S MY CLEAN UNDER-WEAR, FOR PETE'S SAKE?" Pa Loud bellowed. "THE BABY'S EATING OUT OF THE GARBAGE!" Barney Loud shouted.

"WAAAAH!" Baby Loud cried.

On one side of the Loud family lived Miss Shushermush. She didn't like anything loud. She had one quiet fish and wore silent slippers.

"CARE TO JOIN US FOR DINNER?" shouted Pa Loud, as he bang bangity banged his pots and pans.

Bang
Bangity
Bang

"Not tonight," whispered Miss Shushermush. She went inside to eat a quiet meal of leftover mashed potatoes.

On the other side of the Loud family lived Mr. Pitterpatter. He collected china figurines and was not fond of loud bashing and crashing.

"WANNA PLAY CATCH WITH ME?" called Barney Loud, as he thump thumpity thumped his ball against the garage.

"Not right now," sniffed Mr. Pitterpatter. He hurried inside to dust his china.

Behind the Loud family lived Miss Meekerton. She collected pincushions.
It was a very quiet hobby.

"WOULD YOU LIKE SOME SNAPDRAGONS?" hollered
Ma Loud, as she clack clackity clacked her
gardening clippers.

"No thank you," said Miss Meekerton. She
tiptoed inside to count her new pincushions.

CLack

clack

Clack
Clackity
Clack

At night, the Louds had parties where everyone
told loud jokes and laughed—HA HA HA!
And danced—CHA CHA CHA!
And sang—LA LA LA!

Ha
Ha
Ha

Cha
cha
cha

Everyone, that is, except for the neighbors, who never accepted the
Louds' invitations. Miss Shushermush tried telling the Louds to quiet down.
"Please lower your voices," she whispered.

"WHAT DID YOU SAY?" "WHERE'S THE REMOTE, FOR PETE'S SAKE?"
"THE BABY'S EATING BAKED BEANS."
"WAAAAH!"

Mr. Pitterpatter tried calling them on the phone to ask them to be quiet. "WILL SOMEONE PLEASE ANSWER THE PHONE?" "WHO TOOK THE REMOTE, FOR PETE'S SAKE?" "THE BABY'S EATING THE CAT'S FOOD." "WAAAAH!"

Miss Meekerton left them a note in their mailbox.

Please try to be quieter, the note said.

"WHERE DID THIS NOTE COME FROM?" "WHO BROKE THE REMOTE, FOR PETE'S SAKE?" "THE BABY'S EATING AN EARTHWORM."

"WAAAAH!"

After weeks and weeks of this, the neighbors met for the first time ever to discuss the Louds.

"They're upsetting my fish," complained Miss Shushermush.

"My china is always shaking," said Mr. Pitterpatter.

"They're disturbing the plants," said Miss Meekerton. "We'll just have to tell them to be quiet or leave!"

They stormed over to the Louds' and tapped quietly on the door.

No one answered.

They all put their ears to the door,
but they couldn't hear a thing.

"It's awfully quiet in there," said
Mr. Pitterpatter.

"Suspiciously quiet," said
Miss Meekerton.

"Perhaps they've gotten
the hint after all," said
Miss Shushermush.

They gave each
other quiet
high fives.

A week passed. Each day Miss Shushermush listened for the Louds, but she couldn't hear a peep. "This is what I call quiet," she said. Her fish looked bored, so she turned on the television.

Mr. Pitterpatter dusted his china figurines.

He listened for the Louds, but all was quiet.

He bit his thumbnail and frowned.

"Not one single sound," he said.

He turned on the vacuum cleaner

just to have some noise.

Miss Meekerton rearranged her pincushion display. "Kind of spooky, how quiet it is," she said. She could even hear her pins drop. She turned on the radio so she wouldn't have to listen to them dropping all the time.

Another week passed, and still no sound from the Louds.

"It was nice of them to invite me to dinner," Miss Shushermush thought. She told jokes—hee hee hee—to her goldfish.

"I should have played catch with Barney," thought Mr. Pitterpatter.
"He was just being friendly." He danced
—cha cha cha—while he ran the
vacuum cleaner.

"It was nice of her to offer me her flowers," Miss Meekerton thought.
She sang—la la la—along with the radio.

Just when everything was
too quiet for Miss Shushermush,
Mr. Pitterpatter, and Miss
Meekerton, a rumbling, grumbling car turned onto
the block. Slam slammity slam went the Louds' car doors. "WHO'S GOT
THE KEYS?" "I NEED HELP WITH THE LUGGAGE, FOR PETE'S SAKE!" "THE BABY
HAS A DIRTY DIAPER." "WAAAAH!"

"The Louds are back!" shouted the neighbors, as they ran outside.

The Louds ordered in pizza and invited everyone over for dinner. Then they told the neighbors all about their vacation and how they had watched loud fireworks and won a hog-calling contest at the county fair.

Miss Shushermush twittered and tittered, tee hee hee.

Mr. Pitterpatter chewed his pizza, chomp chompity chomp.

Miss Meekerton clattered her dishes, clank clankity clank.

At the end of the meal, they all leaned back in their chairs and let out one very loud . . .